Miller Academy

THE
ROYAL VISIT

Other Orchard Storybooks

A CLIPPER STREET STORY

THE ROYAL VISIT

Bernard Ashley

Illustrated by
Jane Cope

ORCHARD BOOKS
London

First published in Great Britain in 1988 by
ORCHARD BOOKS
10 Golden Square, London W1R 3AF
Orchard Books Australia
14 Mars Road, Lane Cove NSW 2066
Orchard Books Canada
20 Torbay Road, Markham, Ontario 23P 1G6
1 85213 079 2
Typeset in Great Britain by Tradespools Ltd,
Station Approach, Frome, Somerset
Printed in Great Britain by A Wheaton, Exeter

The Clipper Street stories are set
in and around the Greenwich area
of South East London which is
shown on the map overleaf.

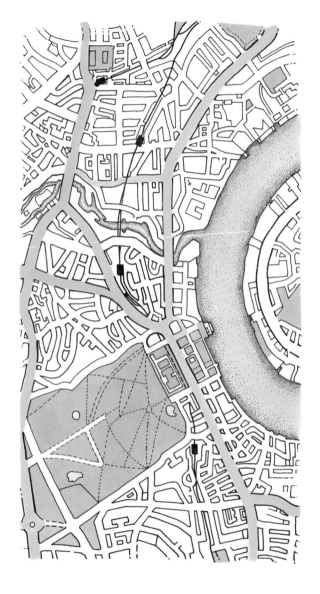

CHAPTER
ONE

The sun shone in through the crinkly glass and dappled on a table. With the pub being closed and empty the dust fell in silence, because the landlord liked it quiet when he was checking a brewer's delivery sheet.

The man from the brewery sat with a coffee while Stevie Bendix made sure about everything before he signed for it.

"Lemonades? Did they go down?"

"You counted them down the cellar yourself. Ten crates. Hundred and twenty."

The publican nodded, as if he'd only been checking for the sake of it. When the trap door to the cellar was open he was there most of the time, standing on the pavement as the barrels and crates slid down the splintery ladder. Now his head was bent low over the sheet picking on the next thing he'd ask about. It paid to keep people on their toes, he always reckoned, or you got taken for a fool now and then.

His head was so low that he couldn't see much of the empty bar—the small tables like islands on the swirly sea of carpet, the round-backed chairs like whalers. And he definitely couldn't see over the horizon, behind the bar.

Which suited Slade a treat: because he might get away with a lot, but he wouldn't get away with this. Not if his father saw him. He'd come in from the back and was crouching down behind the woodwork of the bar. Very carefully he picked up a wine glass by its upturned bottom and crept on his toes along the line of upside-down bottles hanging behind him.

"Gin, gin, gin," he said over and over in his head. But he wasn't much good at printed

words, even when they were the right way up. He knew gin was clear like water, but there were loads of drinks like that. He could easily get the wrong one and there was no way he was going to risk messing up his secret job.

He swore to himself and gave up. He thought for a minute, then he came out and went over to his dad—where he pretended to look down the list he was checking, showing an interest.

"Got enough gin?" he asked. "Nearly out, aren't you?"

It was a brilliant idea. But then he was usually good at getting what he wanted. Stevie Bendix stared round at him. He tapped his pencil on the table and smiled, gave a proud look to the brewery man. "Taking over, are you, son? Won't be long, will it?"

The brewery man tried to look pleased for the lucky old "Yard Arm" pub, having this hard-nosed, spoiled little brat about the place all the time. "Give it ten years he'll be a good little right-hand man. . . ."

"He is now. A devil at school, but a little champeen in here . . ." Slade's father twisted over his shoulder and looked at the line of spirits bottles in their clamps on the wall. "No, we're all right, son. Plenty behind, and that's a good litre up there. See? Second on your left . . ."

Slade looked along the line. "That green bottle?" he asked.

"You've got it."

"Oh, yeah." And the boy strolled away with his father's walk, all hunched shoulders and soft feet.

you, my conscience?" Stevie Bendix had been halfway down a long sum on his calculator and now he wasn't sure whether he'd pressed the last number twice.

"In the middle, left of the till. Filled it up this morning, and there's crates of 'em downstairs." He tutted, and laughed for the brewery man. "Big help!" he said.

Like someone in slow motion Slade lifted a small tonic bottle out of the rack and he put its neck into the opener screwed to the bar. Pressing down, letting the fizz out slowly so it wouldn't sound he uncapped the bottle and tiptoed out with it to where he'd already taken the glass of gin.

CHAPTER THREE

"Yeah, that seems to be in order," Stevie Bendix was saying. "Now, when you coming next week? Don't forget Monday's a bank holiday. . . ."

"Be Tuesday, then. Keep your eye on your stock, though—the way your champeen's drinking the profits you'll need an extra delivery. . . ."

"Eh?" And you could see where Slade got his scowl from. Stevie Bendix looked at the brewery man as if he'd said something well out of order.

"The boy." The man tried a laugh. "Thought you'd seen him. He's took a double gin, then a tonic. For the missus, eh?"

"He's done *what?*"

But even as the brewery man opened his mouth to tell Stevie Bendix what he'd seen, back came Slade, gliding into the bar as quiet as sunlight.

"Yeah, well I'll just check that again. . . ." the publican said in a loud voice. But his eyes were all round the corner, and from then on every move Slade made was being watched in the mirror behind the bar.

Stretching up on his toes to see on the counter, Slade went along the smooth wooden top till he came to the tub where the lemon slices were kept. And moving like a cloud over fields his hand hovered while it quietly prised off the lid. With a thin wooden stick from the egg cup standing near it, his tongue sticking out to keep his mind on what he was doing, Slade stabbed a lemon slice and disappeared with it.

"'Strewth!" said Stevie Bendix. "What's going on?" And with his hands telling the brewery man to stay put, he pushed back his chair and followed to see what the little devil was up to.

CHAPTER
FOUR

He was nowhere to be seen behind the bead curtain. In the kitchen Mrs Bullivant was making sandwiches for the bar snacks—hot marge on a hot knife to spread thin, a filling of square cheese and a spoonful of pickle.

"You seen Slade, have you?"

"No, Mr Bendix." She licked a finger and pressed down hard on a sandwich as if it were the boy.

The publican's eyes skimmed the room for a sight of a glass of gin and tonic. And woe betide her if he saw one because these people knew his rules about drinks on the house.

"Not been through here?"

"Not seen him."

Stevie Bendix backtracked out of the kitchen, went into the cubby-hole of an office where the safe sat. His wife was checking her mouth in a mirror and sorting out the gold on her wrist. She'd be opening up in ten minutes or so.

"Seen Slade?"

"No, thank God."

"Not been in here?"

"Not while I have. Why?"

"Never mind."

Upstairs in the living accommodation a Hoover was worrying at a carpet, up and down, rattling a trapped penny. Like someone out of James Bond, Stevie Bendix jumped in on Doris, nearly did for her in her Walkman.

"You drinking on the job?" he demanded. "You got a gin on the go?"

"Save us!" Doris looked at the ceiling, blew out her last gasp. "I thought me end had come!"

"It will if you're on the booze!" Again, his eyes were seeing glasses everywhere. "Breathe on me," he said.

"Eh?"

Stevie Bendix came close to her. "Breathe on me."

The big woman folded her arms. She was the one person this publican didn't frighten. He gave up the idea.

"You seen Slade?"

"No, it's been a nice mornin'."

He ran round the rest of the rooms. But Slade wasn't in any of the bedrooms and he wasn't locked in the lavatory.

Then where the devil was he? his father worried. With his gin and tonic?

CHAPTER
FIVE

Suddenly it came to him. He knew where the little tyke would be. Where he'd have gone himself as a kid when he was up to something "iffy". The garden shed.

The back of the "Yard Arm" pub wasn't big enough to be a garden for the public. It was just a thin strip of grass with a shed where the lawnmower was kept, along with anything else they didn't have a place for. No one ever went in there except on a search for something. But now Stevie Bendix knew what he would find. He'd open the door and there would be one stupid boy called Slade. An idiot who'd heard people calling for gins and tonics so often he'd decided to try one.

And he'd be down in a corner, sick as a dog, with the mother and father of all headaches and wanting to die. The little fool. But he'd have learned the hard way, and he'd never try it again, his dad knew that.

It was a sensible, sunny morning, but anybody watching from the high flats would have caught a weird sight.

The publican from the "Yard Arm"—the tough guv'nor—coming slinking out of his back door like Tom after Jerry. Then go

creeping on his toes, bent over double, round on the blind side of the garden shed where it had no window. And when he got to the door, going bursting in as if he had a six-gun blazing. Crazy.

"All right, Sladey, what you up to, eh?"

But Slade wasn't up to anything. Because Slade wasn't there. A spider took a scuttle back off its web, and a dying fly started buzzing on the window frame. Nothing else moved, though: and definitely not a green-faced boy.

Saying something best not heard, Stevie Bendix bashed out of the shed and went running back to the pub. He'd give him *champeen*, the little toe-rag!

CHAPTER
SIX

Slade's mother was behind the bar taking the covers off the taps. Ice buckets stood with their lids on in fresh circles of wet. The brewery man was at his table, stapling his sheets and getting impatient for his cheque.

"Won't be a minute, mate. Give him a drink," Stevie instructed his wife. "But where the hell's Slade?"

Lyn Bendix didn't look the least bit concerned. "He's all right. Didn't know you was still looking. He's having a game with a cube of ice. Leave him."

"*Leave him*? I'll. . .! Where is he?"

"Out there." And she nodded at the velvet curtain which led to the side door: the little area which also led to the cellar.

In one short word and a long stride Stevie Bendix was out there—grabbing hard at the shoulder of the boy who was balancing an ice

cube on the palm of his hand and heading for the cellar stairs.

"Come here, you! Slade! What the devil you up to, you little. . . ?"

Slade was spun round by the grab, as near to looking scared as he'd ever done. Perhaps more *awed* than scared.

"Sssh!" he said. "I promised I'd get her drink exactly how she likes it."

"How she likes it?"

"Yeah, you know. Gin, tonic, lemon an' ice. An' this is the ice. I've done it now." Slade held up the melting cube on his wet palm as if his father might not know what ice looked like. "She said, 'I'll have a drink first'."

Stevie Bendix was looking all round him, totally lost as to what the dickens was going on. *"First?"*

"First, before she talks to you." Slade dropped his voice in something like respect. Unheard of. "She wants to see you next."

"See me? Who?" Slade's father scratched

the hair on his chest through his tee shirt. "Who is this, for 'eaven's sake, wants to see me after she's had her blessed gin and tonic?"

Slade looked up at his father with big, important eyes. And he swallowed.

"The Queen!" he said. "You know, *Her*. She's down the cellar!"

CHAPTER
SEVEN

"The Queen?" Stevie Bendix didn't know whether to give Slade a clout or give himself a pinch. This was crazy! The Queen, down the cellar? What monkey business was the little devil up to now? Was he pulling the sort of stunt he pulled at school?

"I'll give you the Queen! Are you looking for a right-hander?" He slapped the ice down out of Slade's palm, sent it skidding across the boards. "Come on, a joke's a joke but stuff a pantomime! What's going on, boy?"

Slade twisted his face at his father—who was nowhere near as important as who was down the cellar. "I told you! It's the Queen. Down there. She's got blue knickers on. . . ."

Now Slade was really close to big trouble. He was expected to be no bother in the school holidays, to help with the glasses and the beer mats. He definitely was not expected to behave like a kid. Stevie Bendix couldn't believe he was actually asking this next question.

"If that's the Queen you've got down there—" he was very close to being hysterical—"how come you know ... *they're blue?*"

"She couldn't help it. It was coming down our trap door. Off the street."

"Off *what?*!" Slade's father clutched at his head.

"She's layin' at the bottom of our ladder. But she's got her gin now. Where's that ice gone?"

"Come down our trap door?" Stevie Bendix yanked Slade up from scrabbling after the ice on the floor. "Save us! Did that stupid fool leave it open?" And, shoving Slade aside, he clattered down the cellar stairs like a stick down railings.

CHAPTER
EIGHT

She did look a bit like the Queen. He could just about give Slade that. She had that sort of face, and a definitely regal look. But it wasn't Her Majesty, and he couldn't figure where the idea had come from. The boy was street wise, not stupid. Blue knickers, even *royal* blue, didn't make anyone the Queen.

But all that could wait. At the top of Stevie Bendix's worries right now was what had happened to this old girl who'd come down through his trap door. Which was shut, so she must've pulled it down on top of her. But had she hurt herself? Because if she had it could cost him a real packet under Health and Safety.

Coming the last bit quietly he looked at her lying there, propped up against the bottom of the delivery ladder—just a thin slit of sun shining down on her tatty hair. With her legs stuck out straight she looked like some human-sized rag doll. Of a novel design. Nodding her head slightly to one side she gave him a look and sipped at her gin.

"Have you brought the ice, Sunshine? I hope you have, 'cos this is the slowest drink I've ever been served. . . ."

Stevie Bendix just swallowed—spit and temper. "Are you all right, love?" he asked quietly. Was she off her rocker? Had she hit her head? Just my luck, he thought. Getting took to court for Health and Safety, for leaving a trap door open. . . . He reached out his hand.

"Don't touch me! Don't move me! Just get me that boy with the ice. Don't he know what's what, getting a drink? I shall have to call a copper. . . ." She looked up towards the trap door, made some feeble movements with her legs: but ended up the same as when she started.

The publican was crouching by her. "Hold on, ma, no need for that. What d'you want— a real nice gin and tonic? The way the guv'nor makes it? Then just don't you move. I'll make you one of my specials, eh?"

Her old head started to nod. "That's

better, mate, that's more like it. Someone with a bit of go, that's what we want." She downed her glass and handed it to Slade's dad. "I can feel the goodness coming back to my legs. But, 'strewth, it was a long way down. . . ."

"There, there. . . ." Stevie Bendix made for the cellar stairs: stopped only to round on Slade. *"The Queen!"* he hissed. "You idiot! Queen of Trouble, more like. Just make sure she don't move. I've gotta keep this one sweet for a bit. . . ."

CHAPTER
NINE

But Slade didn't like being scorned. Not at school and not in the pub. Back here, especially, he liked being Jack-the-lad with his dad.

He slowly approached the old woman. He looked at her shoes, both with holes in them. He looked at her stockings, rumpled up like dead snake skins. He looked at her old lady's dress and her shoddy coat.

And he stood with his feet apart, pulled a face at her and stuck up two fingers. "You!" he twisted from his mouth. "You told me you was the Queen. Why'd you tell me you was the Queen when you ain't?"

The old woman blinked her eyes slowly,

kept her dignity. "Oh—and who said I'm not, then?"

Slade threw his head back, kept his mouth full of the taste of dislike. "My dad. He don't believe me. He don't reckon you are. An' you ain't, are you? He never called you Queen, did he? You were 'aving me over, to get you a drink!"

"Come here," the old woman said. Her voice had gone very low and special, like someone about to share a big secret. "Come over here, son. Go on. Come here. I'll show you something."

Slade wasn't sure. But he couldn't bear not knowing what she was going to show him. Slowly, he moved towards her.

"Come on, come here, close. I can't . . . shout . . . what I'm gonna say. . . ."

Slade moved very close. The way she winked and gave him the come-on this was something very special.

And with a speed and a strength coming from nowhere she suddenly hit him round the head with her bony hand. "I *am* the Queen!" she shouted. "I am the stinkin' Queen! An' don't you never insult an old lady like that again! Queen or not, you don't stick two fingers up at a lady!"

"Ouch! You!" Slade jumped back and swore. He definitely hadn't expected that. And for once he didn't know what to do. If it had been his gran he would have kicked her.

"It don't matter if I'm common as muck. You don't do things like that to me! An' I am the Queen, you little toe-rag. *I am the Queen*!" And suddenly she laughed, a high, gleeful sound. "An' now you can say you've been *crowned* by the Queen! An' you can say 'Thank you, Ma'am,' for the lesson!"

CHAPTER
TEN

Stevie Bendix carried her drink in as if he were a footman at the palace. It was balanced on a not too dented pub tin tray, and by the side of the glass he'd put a small pot of peanuts.

He bent to the old woman and she took the drink without a word. It must have tasted all right because her sip was a good one, with closed eyes. "You can take them peanuts away, with my teeth."

The publican put them on one side—for Slade to work his way through. His own attention was all on the old woman.

"Let's see how you are then, love," he said. "Get up, can you? Put your weight on

your legs?"

The old woman took no notice, wasn't going to be hurried. She made him wait while she took another sip of her drink. "We shall have to see, shan't we?" she said.

After a decent pause, when she'd handed back the glass, Stevie Bendix took her carefully under the arms and lifted her to her feet. By the look of concern on his face she could have been his own old mother being helped up out of a chair.

Slade crunched on the peanuts, leaned back on a barrel. The look on his face said he'd have kicked her to shift her.

"Ups-a-daisy, love," Stevie Bendix was saying. "Take it easy. Now, how's that? All right, are we, eh?"

With one eye on the man, the old woman tested her legs. Not letting go of his shoulder she walked slowly up and down between the crates. Wincing with pain.

"Oo," she said. "Aah. Oh dear." And she lifted her knee like a footballer after a bad tackle. "This leg'll need something. . . ."

And while Slade watched and crunched she went on like that—until, looking her in the eye and nodding, Stevie Bendix slowly put his hand in his left trouser pocket.

CHAPTER
ELEVEN

What he took out was a fat fold of five and ten pound notes. "Perhaps you could buy yourself some ointment with one of these," he said.

She didn't blink. She looked at the money, put her foot to the floor and pulled another face of pain. "Be dear, that would," she said. "It goes deep."

Stevie Bendix came round to stare her in the face. "How deep?" he asked. His voice had changed. It was harder with cash in his hand.

"I dunno." The old woman looked up at the trap door then down at her foot, wiggled it about a bit. "It's a long way down," she said.

"So how much do you reckon it amounts to, the pain of coming that far down?" Slowly, he pulled off one ten pound note and stopped. The old woman said nothing. Off came another. Still not a word: just a drawn-in breath of something sharp catching her. Off came one more ten pound note.

"Dad. . . ." Slade said through a mouthful of peanuts.

"Not now." His father's face was still on the old woman's.

"Good ointment's very dear," she said, her hand half out.

But Stevie Bendix was no stranger to a bit of bribery. All at once he went to put his money away. "Be best if I call a doctor to you, then. Prescriptions are free to old people. . . ."

Still the woman didn't jump too quickly. She kept the same pained look on her face. "No, don't bother no doctor," she said. "They've got enough on. I'll see to myself. Just give us that fifty. . . ."

"Do what? *Fifty?*"

"Or call the doctor if you like. Please yourself. I dunno how I am inside. . . ."

Stevie Bendix swore. And he came up with a different word for every one of the five tenners of the back-hander he peeled off.

"*Dad.* . . ." Slade had come across now and was tugging at his father's arm.

"I said, leave off. I'm doing a bit of business."

"But I'm tellin' you. . . ."

"*Slade!*" Stevie Bendix snapped round hard at his son. "*Shuddup!*"

51

While the old woman took the money and tucked it somewhere very private.

"An' not a word to no one, right, ma?"

"Would I? As if I would. . . . You're a real gentleman. God bless you. . . ."

"Yeah. Heart of gold." But the voice was more like rusted iron.

CHAPTER
TWELVE

When the publican came storming up into the bar the brewery man knew he was in for something. It was the face like a knuckled fist and the eye which didn't waver as he crossed between the tables and chairs.

"You idiot!" Stevie Bendix stormed. "You great idiot! You know what you just cost me?"

Slade had followed his father to the bar, was standing at the end, watching and chewing.

"Wassup? You got what you signed for. . . ." The brewery man was quite big himself, standing up. In his head Slade pictured the chairs and tables going over when it all went off, the way they did some Saturday nights.

"You're s'posed to fix that trap when you're done. Not leave it open for people to fall down!"

"Eh? Who left it open? You sayin' I left it open? You tryin' to cost me my job?" The man took a step towards the publican, moved a chair out of the way himself. "Ask my boy on the wagon."

"Well, didn't you? How come I just had an old girl fall down it?" He took a step forward, too. "I was only lucky she'd settle for a back-hander. Else I could be in all sorts, if she took me to court. . . ."

The men stood eyeing each other. Till all at once the brewery man relaxed. A very knowing look came onto his face. "Hang on," he said. "Did you say an old girl?"

"That's right."

"About sixty, sixty-five?"

"Yeah."

"Tatty hair. Old clothes?"

"Yeah, that's the one. Sladey found her. That's who the drinks was for."

Now Slade was drawn in by his father's look round. He came across the bar and stood by them, nodding. "The Queen, she was — she told me. . . ."

"Yeah." The brewery man sat down. He was nodding, too, and now Slade could see that he was doing his best not to laugh.

"Is she starting it round here? Haven't you heard what's been going on down Thames Reach?"

"No! Heard what?" Mr Bendix perched himself on the edge of a chair.

"She's pulled the same stunt all over, that one. She watches for a delivery, waits till someone's back's turned and she's down their cellar like a shot. Down the ladder real lively, she is. Hides herself in a corner till it's quiet and then sprawls herself out as if she's come pitching down through the open trap. When the cellarman comes back to shoot the bolts, there she is, lying there moaning. . . ."

Stevie Bendix groaned. And Slade, who had been listening to the man without blinking, slowly started backing away. Perhaps if he hadn't his father wouldn't have minded so much, just writing off the fifty pounds to experience. But he knew that innocent look at the ceiling, that little bit of a tune being whistled. Slade never normally whistled anything but abuse.

"Come back here!" his father grabbed his neck. "Come here! What you up to, eh?"

Slade came without a fight. There was no way he ever won once his dad was on to him.

CHAPTER
THIRTEEN

"Come on. What is it? What you been up to?"

Slade set his mouth, sucked at his lower teeth. He really didn't want to say.

"I ain't got all day, boy!"

Still Slade held out. Just for a few moments more. He always timed it to tell just before it was too late.

And now was the moment.

"She looked like the Queen," he said. "Her face. An' she said she was the Queen. That's why I never said. . . ."

"Never said? Never said what? What ain't you told me?"

Slade opened his mouth. Shut it again. Got

ready to duck his head, quick. "I tried to tell you. Down there. I knew she'd never falled. I was ... muckin' about ... an' I saw her come down the ladder. Walking, like, before she laid down...."

"You saw her? *Climbing* down?"

"Yeah—and then she said she was the Queen ... I thought it was ... like ... a visit. You know...."

Stevie Bendix breathed in hard. He was trying to keep hold of something inside, in case he showed himself up. And the brewery man just about kept hold of his laugh.

"You little idiot!" the publican shouted. "Why didn't you *interrupt*? Didn't you see me hand over fifty smackers?"

For once in his life Slade looked near to tears. "Yeah, but she clouted me—an' she still said she was the Queen!"

Stevie Bendix stood up and clutched at the table edge. He made chewing noises at the brewery man. Who, even risking the next explosion, couldn't hold it any longer.

"Sorry, mate," he said, "but your faces. . . ." He sat down, smiling widely and shaking his head. "See, she is the Queen. She never actually tells a lie, that one.

The publican closed his eyes. "Lyn!" he shouted to his wife. "Fetch us something strong, for gawd's sake!"

CHAPTER
FOURTEEN

"The boy's right," the brewery man went on. "She reckons she's the Pearly Queen of Thames Reach. You know the Pearlies. . . ."

Of course Stevie Bendix did; but Slade nodded, too. He'd seen the Pearly Kings and Queens at fairs by the "Cutty Sark" and up on Blackheath—people all dressed in black suits with pearl buttons stitched all over them. In their flat caps and feathers, they were always shaking their collecting boxes for charity.

"Cockney Royal Family, they reckon they are. But not all like her, thank God. Still, she wasn't lying." He eyed Stevie Bendix bravely. "I bet she never actually said she *fell*

down your trap, did she?"

Stevie Bendix stared at Slade: but with eyes that were looking inside, remembering. . . . "No," he muttered, "don't reckon she did, the cunning old. . . ."

"See, as far as anyone's concerned you gave her fifty quid out of the kindness of your heart. . . ."

"Kindness? Daftness, more like. *Stupidity*!" He thumped the table. "An' I don't want this getting round, you hear?"

But now Slade, made right, felt brave enough to come back over and lean an elbow on the table.

"Know what?" he said to his dad, a sudden smart look on his face. "Dunno about white buttons, but it looks like we've been well stitched, you an' me!"

The brewery man stood, still smiling as he put his marked-off delivery notes away.

While Stevie Bendix nodded glumly. "Yeah," he said. "An' in right royal fashion, too. . . ."